Tadpoles

The Wish Fish

by Lynne Benton

Illustrated by Galia Bernstein

FRANKLIN WATTS

First published in 2011 by
Franklin Watts
338 Euston Road
London
NW1 3BH

Franklin Watts Australia
Level 17/207 Kent Street
Sydney
NSW 2000

A CIP catalogue record for this book is available
from the British Library.

ISBN 978 1445 1 0284 9 (hbk)
ISBN 978 1445 1 0290 0 (pbk)

Series Editor: Jackie Hamley
Editor: Melanie Palmer
Series Advisor: Catherine Glavina
Series Designer: Peter Scoulding

Printed in China

Franklin Watts is a division of
Hachette Children's Books,
an Hachette UK company.
www.hachette.co.uk

Ozzie Otter
caught a fish.

4

"I'm a wish fish,"
it said.

Then it swam away.

Three more otters
came along.

"I caught a wish fish,"
said Ozzie.

"But it swam away before I made a wish."

"We'll find it," they said.

But the fish
had gone.

"Never mind. Let's play."
they said.

16

"What did you want to wish for?" they asked.

"Friends to play with!"
Ozzie smiled.

Puzzle Time!

Put these pictures in the right order and tell the story!

shy

lucky

magical

lonely

Which words describe Ozzie and which describe the wish fish?

Turn over for answers!

Notes for adults

TADPOLES are structured to provide support for newly independent readers. The stories may also be used by adults for sharing with young children.

Starting to read alone can be daunting. **TADPOLES** help by providing visual support and repeating words and phrases. These books will both develop confidence and encourage reading and rereading for pleasure.

If you are reading this book with a child, here are a few suggestions:

1. Make reading fun! Choose a time to read when you and the child are relaxed and have time to share the story.
2. Talk about the story before you start reading. Look at the cover and the blurb. What might the story be about? Why might the child like it?
3. Encourage the child to retell the story, using the jumbled picture puzzle as a starting point. Extend vocabulary with the matching words to characters puzzle.
4. Give praise! Remember that small mistakes need not always be corrected.

Answers

Here is the correct order:

1.c   2.f   3.a   4.e   5.b   6.d

Words to describe Ozzie: lonely, shy

Words to describe the wish fish: lucky, magical